Leo's Skiing Surprise

Leo's Skiing Surprise

Louise Leblanc

Illustrated by Jules Prud'homme
Translated by Sarah Cummins

First Novels

Formac Publishing Company Limited
Halifax, Nova Scotia

Originally published as *Un vampire en détresse*
Copyright © 2000 Les éditions de la courte échelle inc.
Translation copyright © 2007 Sarah Cummins

Formac Publishing Company Limited recognizes the support of the
Province of Nova Scotia through the Department of Tourism, Culture and
Heritage. We acknowledge the financial support of the Government of
Canada through the Book Publishing Industry Development Program
(BPIDP) for our publishing activities.

Formac Publishing Company Limited acknowledges the support of the
Canada Council for the Arts for our publishing program.

NOVA SCOTIA
Tourism, Culture and Heritage

Canada Council   Conseil des Arts
for the Arts   du Canada

Library and Archives Canada Cataloguing in Publication

Leblanc, Louise, 1942-
[Un vampire en détresse. English]
   Leo's skiing surprise / Louise Leblanc ; illustrations by Jules
Prud'homme ; translated by Sarah Cummins.

(First novels 62)
Translation of: Un vampire en détresse.
ISBN 978-0-88780-738-1 (bound).--ISBN 978-0-88780-736-7 (pbk.)

   I. Prud'homme, Jules II. Cummins, Sarah III. Title.
IV. Title: Vampire en détresse. English. V. Series.

PS8573.E25V3513 2007   jC843'.54   C2007-904110-8

Formac Publishing Company Ltd.
5502 Atlantic Street
Halifax, Nova Scotia, B3H 1G4
www.formac.ca

Printed and bound in Canada

Table of Contents

1

The Message

I have the coolest friend! His name is Julio Orasul and he's a vampire. He lives with his parents in an underground apartment in the cemetery.

Julio and I keep in touch by leaving messages on my grandfather's gravestone.

Unfortunately, we can't get together very often. Julio can't go out in the daytime, because the light would kill him. And we have to be careful. The Orasuls could be in danger if people in the village found out about them.

My family and Mr. Applebaum know about the Orasuls. They've helped me think of ways to get Julio involved in things. Being a vampire is hard on him. He wishes he were free to try new activities.

I have a special Christmas present in mind for him. It would be so exciting! The only problem is convincing his parents.

I'm writing to Julio now so we can get together and figure it out.

Julio—

Meet me at the cemetery tomorrow

night at nine. I'll be with Mr.

Applebaum. Tell your parents he

would like to meet them. It's about

your Christmas present, which is

totally cool! You're going to love it!

Leo

2

The Gift of Freedom

Great leaping french fries! I never thought my parents would flip out like this.

"Leo, you have no idea how dangerous this outing would be!"

"We couldn't take responsibility for something like this!"

"Don't worry!" I told them. "Mr. Applebaum will take responsibility. He's meeting the Orasuls tomorrow. If they agree, I don't see why you would say no!"

I'm generally a pretty easygoing guy, but I turn into a lion when I'm defending Julio. My parents were speechless.

"I'm off," I announced, "to deliver my message to Julio."

Pleased with my victory, I went to put on my jacket. As I was about to open the door, I heard my mother say, "I'm going to call Mr. Applebaum. He mustn't get involved in this."

"Oh, let it be," my dad answered. "The Orasuls will never agree to it anyway."

That shook me up. I was a humbled lion, dragging my tail. Outside, it was freezing and I felt even more depressed.

"Hey, Leo! You're just the guy I wanted to talk to."

Oh no! It was Butch, the school bully. He was a big kid, fourteen years

old, and he always seemed ready to attack. But he hadn't bothered me for a while, so I wasn't as afraid of him as I used to be.

"We have nothing to say to each other, Butch."

"Come on! Five minutes. Let's have a hot dog at Mick's. My treat!"

The nerve! If he thinks he can make up for all the misery he's caused me by buying me a stupid hot dog! He can beg all he wants, I'll still say no.

"Leave me alone, Butch," I said, walking away. "Quit bugging me."

"I could really bug you, if that's the way you want it," he growled.

I stopped, despite myself. I began to feel afraid again. Fear was like the tip of an iceberg in the pit of my stomach. More and more of the iceberg rose up as the footsteps behind me came closer. A hand fell onto my shoulder, like a ton of ice.

***

I chewed my hot dog slowly, while Butch gobbled his.

"Bring us a couple more," he called to Mick. "I'm loaded today," he added to me, with a funny look.

"I don't really care, Butch. Just say what you have to say."

"Okay, all right. I want to ask you a favour. I'd like you to deliver a letter."

He took out an envelope with a name written on it. Great leaping french fries! It was for Julio!

Butch had met him with Mr. Applebaum at the school one evening. Mr. Applebaum had told him that Julio was his nephew, and that he was seriously ill. That was to explain how pale Julio was.

"I though Julio might come visit his uncle at Christmas," said Butch. "I'd like to see him again. I'm sure he'll say yes after he reads my letter."

No way! I'd never let Julio fall into Butch's hands! My inner lion was awakened.

"I'm not your mailman."

"Well, tell me Julio's address, then."

My inner lion panicked.

"His a … a … address?"

"Yes, his address! If you don't give it to me, Leo, I might take it the wrong way."

I felt queasy, like the hot dog was coming back up my throat. Butch made me sick.

"No!" I yelled at him. "You won't make me! I don't even know Julio's address, and I'm sick and tired of your bullying!"

"Whoa!" Mick called to me from behind the counter. "And you, Butch, stop picking on that kid."

Like a hunted animal, I skittered away while Butch defended himself.

"I wasn't picking on him! I've never

been so polite in my life! The kid is crazy!"

I ran straight to the cemetery. I had to talk to Granddad. He always answers my call. His voice speaks to me from beyond the grave. Honest! It's true. I'm not crazy!

"Granddad, are you there?"

"I'm heeeeere, Leeeo. Where else would I be?"

His warm chuckle already made me feel better. I told him everything — my plan for Julio's present, my parents' reaction, and now this thing with Butch.

"I've had it up to here with other people, Granddad. At least I've got you."

"I'd come and join you if I could,

kid. I miss living, even with other people. It can be awful, but it can also be great."

"Right now it's awful."

"Well," he told me, "the darkest hour is just before dawn. Your plan might work out. You should leave your message for Julio."

***

It was a good thing I listened to Granddad. Mr. Applebaum managed to convince my parents. When Julio came to meet me, I told him about the present.

"For Christmas, I want you to feel as free and as fast as the wind. Your present is a night of skiing at Beaumont!"

Julio's eyes sparkled with joy. But

then the lights went out, like on a Christmas tree when you pull the plug.

"My parents will never let me," he said.

Five minutes later, his prediction came true.

"Never!" Julio's mother cried.

"Think about what could happen if there is an accident," his father added.

Mr. Applebaum tried to reassure them, but it was no good. The Orasuls would not budge.

"Skiing is not for vampires. Period."

"It's not true!" Julio burst out. "Our cousins in Beaumont go skiing. And snowmobiling too! They go to the movies. They're modern vampires!"

"They are mistaken vampires, who think they can escape from our world,"

declared Mrs. Orasul.

"They're only trying to improve their lives," said Mr. Applebaum. "It's a hard life for young people."

"You're telling me!" muttered Julio, dejected.

3

More Scared Than Hurt

"Jingle BELLS! Jingle BELLS! Jingle all the way!"

"Oh what FUN it is to ride in a one-horse open sleigh!"

"HEY!"

"Quiet down!" yelled Mr. Applebaum. "I can't hear myself drive! I promised your parents we would be extremely careful, Julio. They finally agreed to let you come, because they love you. So, cut the silliness."

Julio became serious. Great leaping french fries, we're supposed to be having fun, not torturing ourselves!

"No worries," I joked. "Julio's mom wrapped him up like a package mailed to the North Pole."

"That reminds me," said Mr. Applebaum. "Someone gave me a letter for you, Julio."

Uh-oh. It can't be! Not …

"It was Butch McGee. It seemed very important to him."

"He's still so lonely," Julio said sympathetically.

My claws came out. "You're not going to see him, are you?"

"I don't think that was what the

letter was about," said Mr. Applebaum. "Butch told me he was going away, to visit his uncle who has a cabin in the woods. Near Beaumont, actually."

I was surprised and relieved.

"Good riddance," I said. "He won't be around to cause problems."

Julio took the letter and put it in his pocket.

"We'll be there soon!" announced Mr. Applebaum.

***

We had been skiing for an hour, and Julio was still as thrilled as the first time he'd zoomed down the slopes.

"Ah, free in nature. I'm high on skiing!"

"Just don't lose sight of the track," Mr. Applebaum said. "You're straying too far from the lighted areas."

"You're forgetting that a vampire is like a bat, a creature of the night," Julio teased him.

"Well, I have to keep near you, and I'm not a bat," Mr. Applebaum replied. "Okay, time for a break."

He led us back to the car and took out a thermos Mrs. Orasul had given him.

Julio made a face. "It's probably one of her horrible vitamin potions."

"A potion for bats!" Mr. Applebaum laughed. "Come on. I'll treat you to a human-style meal."

While we stuffed our faces at the restaurant, Julio looked around at all the people.

"It would be fun if we ran into

Horatio and Bella, my cousins from Beaumont. They're great!"

"According to your mother, they are wild vampire kids," Mr. Applebaum reminded him.

"She's afraid I'll want to act like them," said Julio.

"She's probably right to be worried," remarked Mr. Applebaum. "You're quite the daredevil. So please, be careful!"

We hurried back to the slopes. Time was flying, way too fast for us! When Mr. Applebaum waved to us that it was time to go, Julio caught my eye and pointed to the ski lift. We dashed over and jumped on.

Once we were in the air, I looked back. Mr. Applebaum was seated a few places behind us. I suddenly felt bad at how stupid we had been. Julio said nothing, but looked guilty. The wind was blowing harder now, making the seats sway.

I was relieved when we reached the top. Julio took off right away, calling, "I'm too embarrassed to face Mr. Apple—."

He fell over, got up again, and was off.

Then Mr. Applebaum was there, setting off after Julio. My legs felt shaky, but I followed. On the way down, I kept praying. No, nothing had happened. At the last turn … great leaping french fries! A small crowd had gathered.

I hurried over, dreading the worst.

"He's more scared than hurt," Mr. Applebaum said.

My worry disappeared, along with the last bit of strength in my legs. My heart fluttered, my knees gave way, and I felt myself falling, falling …

4

It's Coming Closer … It's Stopping!

Safe and warm in the car, I explained, "I felt like I was falling off the mountain. I thought I was going to die."

"I really did go tumbling down the mountain," said Julio. "I can't believe I'm still alive."

We laughed nervously. There was no reaction from Mr. Applebaum. He hadn't opened his mouth from the minute we got in the car. Julio tried to make peace by repeating his own words.

"In the end, I guess we were more scared than hurt!"

"It's worse than that," grumbled Mr. Applebaum. "We lost a lot of time. The weather has turned bad. If we had left earlier, we would have missed this blizzard."

A blizzard! I peered out the window. All right, it was snowing, but not that much. Julio looked at me fearfully. I made a reassuring sign, then a clump of snow hit the car window and made me jump.

Mr. Applebaum drove in silence, watching the road. The wind picked up, blowing gusts of snow across the road. It was hard to see.

He slowed down and kept driving. It was like riding a tortoise who doesn't care about winning the race, as long as he gets to the finish line.

Still, I thought Mr. Applebaum was being a bit too cautious. We had just reached a clear spot. He could speed up a bit!

A car passed us and then disappeared like a ghost. A second later, a wave of powdery snow swallowed us up. We were plunged into the middle of a whirlwind, drowning in a white ocean of snow.

We couldn't see a thing! Mr. Applebaum braked and the car began to skid. AIIIEEE!

We were heading towards the ditch!

I grabbed Julio's hand to say goodbye.

***

It was dark. I was lost … in a nightmare. That's right. I was waking

up from a nightmare. AIIIEEE! Then I
remembered—the accident! I relived
every second in fast-motion.

"JULIO! MR. APPLEBAUM!"

They must be dead! In a panic, I felt
around me in the emptiness.

"Calm down, Leo. It's all right.

You can move, and so can I. Julio is right here beside me, and he's breathing. We've got to get some light."

Mr. Applebaum's voice brought me back from the grave. I began to make out shapes in the darkness, then I heard a groan. Julio was coming to! I heard a click, and light flooded from a flashlight.

I just wanted to be with Julio.

The car was tilted. I grabbed the back of the seats and squeezed between the two front seats. Mr. Applebaum was examining Julio.

"Nothing seems to be broken,"

"My head hurts," groaned Julio. Mr Applebaum took a look.

"It's just a little cut," he said

comfortingly. Still, he hurriedly made a bandage from his scarf.

"I'm going to get out to look for help. My door is blocked, so I'll have to get out the other one. We'll have to move Julio to the back."

I helped him as best I could, with my aches and pains. When Julio and I were snug in the back seat, Mr. Applebaum still seemed worried.

"The blanket there! You have to wrap up," he whispered.

Suddenly, the sound of an engine covered his voice, a rumbling noise that instantly faded into the distance. But Mr. Applebaum was cheered.

"A snowmobile! The track must run alongside the forest here. I'm going to take a look."

He crawled over and opened the door. Snow poured into the car. This cruel reminder of the blizzard outside dashed my spirits.

What did Mr. Applebaum think he would find? There wouldn't be another snowmobile. The first one had probably been ambushed by the storm, like us. You'd have to be crazy to go out in weather like this. I sank again into misery and exhaustion.

"LEO! JULIO!"

It was Mr. Applebaum! He'd made it back to the car!

"I managed to open the trunk, and I put some flares at the side of the road," he announced. "I also found the thermos."

Mrs. Orasul's vitamin potion tasted

awful, but it did seem to give all three of us new strength. For now, anyway.

I gradually slipped into sleep. Delirious, I tried to call my grandfather, but my mother answered: "You have no idea how dangerous this outing would be!" Then I heard another scolding voice—Butch's! His hand came down on my shoulder. No!

"Leo! It's me!"

I recognized Mr. Applebaum's voice and returned to the real world.

"Did you hear that? An engine! A snowmobile! It's coming closer … it's stopping!"

He crawled to the front of the car, opened his window, and began to wave the flashlight around.

A few moments later, a face

appeared at the window. No! It couldn't be! I was hallucinating again.

5

You're Totally Bonkers, Leo!

"I want the truth, Butch." Mr. Applebaum was losing patience. "Your uncle would not have let you go out in weather like this."

Then Butch told us a terrible story. First, he had stolen some money from his father.

I remembered his words in the restaurant: "I'm loaded today."

His father had found out and smacked him around. Then he sent him to his brother's. And the brother was just as bad.

"He didn't suspect anything when I went out," said Butch. "I would rather face the snowstorm than him."

"I understand," murmured Mr.

Applebaum. "I'll look after you, I promise. But first we've got to get out of here. The road is closed. There's no light from that side. So tell me, does your uncle have another snowmobile?"

"He's got a bunch more. He runs the repair shop, you know, where the tracks cross."

"I'll go over there and come back with him. We'll need two snowmobiles to get us out of here."

"I won't stay, then. I don't want to see him again."

"You don't need to worry. I'll be there. Trust me," he added. "Just like I trust you to watch over Julio and Leo."

"Is Julio here?" exclaimed Butch. "I didn't recognize him."

"Hi, Butch," said Julio weakly.

"Thanks for stopping."

His words transformed Butch. He seemed to take charge of the situation.

"I brought a thermal blanket and some things to eat," he said. "I'll go get them."

"Good! I'll meet you at the snowmobile," said Mr. Applebaum. "I won't be gone long, kids. Be brave!"

Different emotions swept over me. I felt helpless. And I resented Butch. Who did he think he was? Our saviour? I can watch over Julio without his help!

But … I could hardly stand up, I was so bent and bruised. A blast of icy air sent me shivering under the covers again.

It was the saviour returning!

"Good news! The storm is dying down a bit. And I have what we need to

get you guys warmed up."

Butch mixed some powder into a thermos and passed it to me. I wanted to turn it down, but my body cried out for help. I sipped at the steaming soup and it brought my strength back.

Butch bent over Julio and then pulled back. Blood was running down Julio's forehead. I sat up in horror.

"I know what to do," said Butch.

"Don't take the scarf off, whatever you do."

He took a pocket knife out of his bag, clenched it between his teeth, and jumped out of the car.

I couldn't move. I was paralyzed with fear. The blood kept trickling down Julio's face. Panic swept over me. I began to shake, as if I could feel death coming.

"Move over, Leo!" It was Butch. I hadn't heard him coming.

He was carrying a slab of ice. He broke it up with his knife and held a thick layer of ice cubes against Julio's forehead.

Following his lead, I began to get hold of myself. I handed Butch my scarf to make a second bandage. I filled the thermos lid with soup.

"Good idea," said Butch. The hot liquid revived Julio.

"Mmmm … I feel … come back … far away. You …"

"We've got to keep talking to him," said Butch, "so he'll stay conscious."

"You scared us, you know, Julio," I said. "Especially me!"

"… guys are great …"

"*You're* great," said Butch. "I wrote you that in my letter."

"Your letter? Oh, right … I haven't had time to read it yet."

"I know it by heart. I started it at least ten times! Listen! Uh, yeah, here goes:

> *Julio, when I first met you, you were*
>
> *kind to me. I thought you were*

great. Before meeting you, I thought

that there was no such thing as

goodness. You have lit a little

candle in my life, which is filled

with darkness. I …

Butch was talking to Julio as he would to a friend. He seemed so helpless, suddenly. I didn't know what to think of him anymore. I was confused....

I slipped into the front seat to stretch my legs and clear my mind. I felt a bit stronger, so I opened the window.

The wind did seem to have died down a bit. I could hear … great leaping french fries! Two snowmobiles. They were stopping! It couldn't be Mr.

Applebaum — he had just left.

"Someone's here!" I said.

I grabbed the flashlight and leaned out the window. Shadows came closer. I turned the light on and shone it out.

"Is it my uncle?" asked Butch, worried.

"No, it's … SANTA CLAUS!"

"Now you've gone totally bonkers, Leo!" cried Butch.

***

If anyone was bonkers, it was our visitors, a couple disguised as Santa Claus and a fairy princess. They had just wanted to surprise their little cousin — in the middle of a blizzard! Totally bonkers.

They offered to drive us to shelter, but we explained that Mr. Applebaum

would soon be back. They decided to stay with us until he returned.

"You never know," said the fairy princess.

I invited them to sit and wait in the car. Santa Claus offered to take a look at Julio.

"You put ice on. That's good, it stopped the bleeding. But ... hey! It's ..."

Why was he patting Julio's face like that?

"Julio! Wake up! It's me, Horatio! Your cousin from Beaumont!"

The famous vampire Julio had told me about!

"Julio is unconscious. There's no time to lose. He needs bl—a blood transfusion. I know his blood type is V2, like his parents. Quick!"

There was no way of stopping Horatio. He was determined. I realized what *V2* meant: Julio needed *"Vampire Type 2"* blood. But how could I explain that to Butch? He didn't know that Julio was a …

"Julio needs special blood!" cried Butch. "Because he's a … because of his illness, right? We have to save him, Leo! You go with him. I'll stay here and wait for Mr. Applebaum. If he comes back and finds the car empty, he'll think the worst has happened. So you go!"

***

"If all goes well, we'll be at the Orasuls' in less than an hour," Horatio said.

He had put Julio onto a kind of sled

51

attached to the back of his snowmobile. I climbed onto the other snowmobile behind Bella, the fairy princess. We set off.

The cold chilled me to the bone. I began to wish I had stayed in the car. But then I thought of Butch, staying behind alone. Knowing that his uncle would be coming. So much courage … all to save Julio. I was ashamed of my weakness.

Then the track went into a forest, out of the wind. We were wrapped in a hushed silence, as the huge pine trees slept under their blankets of snow. They seemed to jump awake as they were lit by our headlights.

The snowmobiles raced along like satellites in a world of frozen ghosts. I

had a feeling this voyage would never end, that we would not be able to win the race against ... death.

Suddenly we came out of the forest onto a lake. I could tell the blizzard was now behind us. Horatio took advantage of the flat surface to speed up.

His snowmobile sped off into the distance. As it grew smaller, it seemed to climb into the sky. To my eyes, it looked like the silhouette of Santa's sleigh.

I had a crazy thought. If I made a wish with all my being, then Santa Claus would make the wish come true.

"I beg you, Santa Claus, for just one last present. Save Julio's life! If you do, I'll never ask you for anything ever again!"

6

You Were Right, Granddad!

After it was all over, Bella drove me
home. I still didn't know if Julio was
all right.

At home, I slept. I wanted to forget
everything. At four o'clock, my mother
came to wake me up.

"We have to go to the Orasuls',
Leo."

I didn't want to go. I was afraid I
would find out I'd lost my friend
forever.

"Do you hear, Leo? Mr. Applebaum
is here."

Like a zombie, I followed my

mother to the living room.

"When the road opened again, I came back with Butch in a taxi," Mr. Applebaum told us. "I warned his parents that I would take action to protect him. I intend to report his situation to …"

Mr. Applebaum's words were swept away by the storm in my head. I felt weak and dizzy.

"It's time to leave now," my dad said.

He gently shook my shoulder and led me to the car. We drove through the cemetery to the Orasuls' tomb. We went down the steps leading to their apartment. My head was spinning. The door opened …

Great leaping french fries! Julio! He

had opened the door! I fell into his
arms and burst into tears.

***

Once things had calmed down, the
Orasuls told us Julio's life had been saved
by the blood transfusion. That's all they
said. It was as if they wanted to keep
certain vampire secrets to themselves.

I wanted to share my own secret. I
told them all that I had begged Santa

Claus to save Julio, and he had given me my wish.

From their shocked faces, I could tell I should have kept my secret to myself.

"I meant Horatio!" I added hastily. "He was Santa Claus."

"Butch was the real Santa," said Horatio. "If he hadn't put ice on the wound, Julio would have bled to death."

"Who is this young man?" asked Mr. Orasul. Mr. Applebaum told him about Butch.

"Sometimes he does stupid things, because he's left to run wild too much," he said in conclusion. "But he has some fine qualities."

"The main thing is that he saved my

son," said Mr. Orasul. "I would like to express my gratitude."

"He can't come here!" Mrs. Orasul cried. "He is unstable and cannot be trusted."

"Right, Mom!" Julio was outraged. "We can't trust him or Horatio or Bella or any of those wild young people on their snowmobiles who played Santa for me!"

Julio's mom turned red … Santa Claus red.

"Don't worry, Aunt Anna," Bella laughed. "We know how you worry. But I can assure you that we are always very careful. We do go out in the daytime, but only at dawn."

At that, Mrs. Orasul turned white again … vampire white.

"I would like to invite you all to a less dangerous event," my mother proposed. "Christmas Eve supper!"

"Shall we ask Butch, too?" suggested Mr. Applebaum. "You can thank him then."

Everyone thought that was a great idea. Even Mrs. Orasul.

***

Before leaving the cemetery, I went to visit Granddad.

"I understand now why you miss life, Granddad," I told him. "When you get a glimpse of death up close like I did, afterwards you realize how cool it is to be alive."

"Enjoy it, kid!"

"You were also right about other people. There's both good and bad in

people. Butch was great! The only thing is … that bugs me! I feel bad about myself."

"Are you afraid that Julio will become friends with Butch? Didn't you want to offer him the gift of freedom? Now's the time. If you're really his friend, you can let him decide."

"I am really his friend. For life, and to the death! But you're right, Granddad. I'll let Julio decide. But I hope he'll decide not to tell Butch his address."

Hearing Granddad's warm chuckle, I already felt better. I was ready to have a merry and peaceful Christmas!

Fred and the Pig Race
By Marie-Danielle Croteau
Illustrated by Bruno St-Aubin

Fred is going to spend the weekend of the Saint Yaya agricultural fair with his friend William. This year, William and his pig Omer are going to participate in the big race. Unfortunately, on the morning of the race, William is sick. Fred quickly decides to replace him. But how can he win the race when he has never ridden a pig?

This hilarious story shows that telling the truth is always the best idea.

Raffi's Animal Rescue
By Sylvain Meunier
Illustrated by Élisabeth Eudes-Pascal

Raffi McCaffrey can't move the way most kids can. He has a condition that makes it hard for him to get around. So, he spends a lot of time at his window watching the birds. One morning, when he is studying the trees outside his window, he suddenly sees something move. It's a bird — and it's injured! Its wing is hurt and it can't fly any more. What can Raffi do to save the bird?

In this story readers will learn about ways of coping with disabilities.